Tracy Kane

Tracy Kane studied illustration
in Philadelphia and London, England.
She lives in New Hampshire with
her husband, Barry, and
their cat, Toulouse.

After working as a commercial
artist for Public Television, she now
spends most of her time illustrating
and painting, drawing upon
New England's scenery as
inspiration for her work.

Tracy was the type of child who
loved exploring the outdoors,
and she still finds it easy to
believe in Nature's magic!

....

Fairy Boat is a member
of the award-winning
Fairy Houses Series
of books created by Tracy Kane.

Fairy Boat

by Tracy Kane

The Fairies would like to thank
Barry Kane and **Patricia Sullivan**
who have sprinkled their talents like
fairy dust throughout these pages.

Chelsea awoke early and tiptoed to her grandfather's workshop.
She picked out a brush and carefully began to paint letters on a
small sailboat sitting atop the workbench. Her grandfather had made the
boat from leftover scraps of maple and ash. Her grandmother had bought
fabric in Chelsea's favorite colors to sew the sails. Now it was Chelsea's
turn. Her job was to paint the name she had chosen for the boat.
The paint had to be dry by that afternoon...

...for this was the day "Fairy Boat" would be launched.

Grandpa and Gram's house bordered a small stream that wound its way through the woods before widening into a river.

Chelsea and her friend, Kristen, had built fairy houses in these woods using twigs, bark, leaves and other pieces of nature. That's how Chelsea came up with "Fairy Boat," a perfect name, she thought, a magical name that might even entice a few fairies to take a sailboat ride.

"Look, Gram!" Chelsea exclaimed. "Some fairies are following my boat!"

"Yes, I do think I see something," Gram said, squinting into the bright sun.
A strong breeze filled Fairy Boat's sails. Her colors sparkled in the sun as
she began to glide faster downstream. "Let's get a closer look and then
pick her up before she rounds the bend into the river," said Grandpa.
"Then we can go back upstream and put her in again."

A mother goose nesting on the riverbank spied
the boat bobbing toward her nest.

"Uh oh," Grandpa said, that
goose thinks Fairy Boat is after her eggs."

"She's chasing our boat out to the river!" Chelsea
shouted over the honking and flapping.

As the current carried Fairy Boat further and further
downstream, Gram scrambled after her as fast as she could.
"I think I can still grab her!" she said.

But the goose was faster.

"Well *someone* likes our boat!" exclaimed Gram, who was first around the bend.

A pair of otters were playing with the boat like a bath toy. They flipped and splashed and spun in the water, pushing the boat toward the lily marsh where the river widened.

"Oh dear," Grandpa sighed as Fairy Boat bobbled into the marsh. "She's well beyond our reach now."

Chelsea felt her heart sink. "But what will happen to Fairy Boat? Will we ever see her again?"

Grandpa tried to look cheerful. "There's a chance she'll get caught up on something, maybe end up grounded." Then he lowered his voice. "But if she doesn't get stuck, the journey down river is a couple of miles."

"A couple of miles is a great distance for a little boat like that," Gram said gently. "I'm afraid Fairy Boat is on her own now, Chelsea. She'll have to fend for herself."

As the sun sank lower in the sky, Gram's thoughts turned to dinner.
She'd planned to bake a pie for dessert, so she needed to get started.
"It's time we headed home," she said.

Later, even though blueberry was her favorite pie, Chelsea felt sad that she would never see Fairy Boat again.
Night had settled in, and she wondered whether boats might be afraid of the dark.

"You know, Fairy Boat won't be alone," Chelsea said, as Gram tucked her into bed. "The fairies will keep her company. Besides... she's very brave." She yawned sleepily and snuggled more deeply under her blanket.

"Sweet dreams," Gram said as she kissed Chelsea goodnight.

The next morning, Chelsea sprang out of bed. "Where do you suppose Fairy Boat is now, Gram?"

"Hmmm... Let me think." Gram said. "If she stayed afloat through the night,
then she faces great danger ahead. Remember the old mill in town?
The river turns into a steep waterfall there as it pours over the town dam.
I don't think our little boat can survive that fall
without being crushed."

"But Grandpa built her to be strong, Gram. She won't sink."

Chelsea shut her eyes tightly as she spoke, trying to imagine Fairy Boat sailing upright over the dam.

Chelsea felt a comforting hand on her shoulder and looked up at Grandpa. "Chelsea, if Fairy Boat somehow does make it over the falls intact, she'll be floating in salt water as she heads for the harbor. She'll have to dodge all the large boats mooring there and hope they don't squash her."

"Oh," Chelsea said, her voice falling.
Then she brightened. "Hey! Fairy Boat is
so little she could sneak right past them!"

"If she did make it past the boats," Gram said, thinking aloud, "she'd have to sail past Seal Rocks, where the bay empties into the ocean."

"The sea can get very rough, with huge waves. The changing tides and winds could blow her miles and miles from any land at all."

"The Fairies will protect her," Chelsea said quietly.
"If they need to, they could even use magic
to get her back to shore."

"You never know," Gram replied.

Earlier in the week, Chelsea's grandparents had promised her a trip to the ocean. Now was the time to make good on that promise, Gram thought.

She packed a picnic of
sandwiches, plums, and
cookies, and the three
of them headed out.

As they drove to the beach, Chelsea looked at a map that Grandpa gave her. They were headed to Catchall Cove.

Gram and Grandpa's House

Goose Nest

Fairy Woods

Firefly Fields

Otter Bend

Lily Marsh

Beaver Lodge

Turtle Log

Map of
Big River

Old Mill
Town

Catchall
Cove

Ocean

Harbor

Seal Rocks

Chelsea loved beachcombing.

She never knew what treasures
the sea might wash ashore.

Have you found all the
fairies who appear in this story?

Some of us are easy to find,
but many of us are hidden!

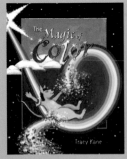